OLIVIA™

Helps the Tooth Fairy

By Cordelia Evans
Illustrated by Jared Osterhold

SIMON SPOTLIGHT
An imprint of Simon & Schuster Children's Publishing Division
New York   London   Toronto   Sydney   New Delhi
1230 Avenue of the Americas, New York, New York 10020
First Simon Spotlight paperback edition May 2015
OLIVIA™ Ian Falconer Ink Unlimited, Inc. and © 2015 Ian Falconer and Classic Media, LLC.
All rights reserved, including the right of reproduction in whole or in part in any form. SIMON SPOTLIGHT and
colophon are registered trademarks of Simon & Schuster, Inc. For information about special discounts for bulk
purchases, please contact Simon & Schuster Special Sales at 1-866-506-1949 or business@simonandschuster.com.
Manufactured in the United States of America 0415 LAK   2 4 6 8 10 9 7 5 3 1
ISBN 978-1-4814-1906-2   ISBN 978-1-4814-1907-9 (eBook)

"How was school today?" Mother asked Olivia and Ian.

"Great!" said Olivia as she disappeared up the stairs.

"Wonderful, sweetheart," Mother called after her. "And Ian, how was your day?"

Ian looked up at her glumly.

"I'm one of the only kids in my class who hasn't lost a tooth yet!" Ian blurted out. "My teacher has a chart on the wall, and every time you lose a tooth, she puts a sticker up next to your name. Some kids have four stickers, and I have zero!"

Mother gave Ian a big hug. Everyone loses their teeth at different times—yours are just taking a little longer," she said. "And besides, I thought your front tooth was loose!"

"It is," Ian admitted. "But when will it will fall out?"

"It'll be out before you know it," promised Mother. "Just be patient."

Later that afternoon Olivia went into the kitchen to get a snack, and found Ian sitting at the table eating a bowl of honey.

"That's an interesting snack, Ian," she commented. "Do you even like honey?"

"No, but I'm trying to eat sticky things so that my loose tooth comes out," Ian explained.

"Oh, so you can get a sticker on the chart at school?" asked Olivia. "Don't worry, Ian! Pretty soon you'll have lots of stickers up there!"

"It's not just that," said Ian. "I heard that after your tooth comes out, if you put it under your pillow, the Tooth Fairy will come and leave you a present!"

"That's true," said Olivia.

"Well, I want a visit from the Tooth Fairy!" Ian replied. "I wonder if the Tooth Fairy would leave me a robot . . ."

Olivia and Ian imagined what it
would be like if the Tooth Fairy put a
robot under Ian's pillow.

"I don't think she leaves presents quite that big. She usually leaves a quarter or some change," said Olivia.

"That's okay," said Ian. "I'd be happy with any size present. I just really want the Tooth Fairy to come!"

That night as she lay in bed trying to fall asleep, Olivia kept thinking about Ian and his tooth. She really wanted to do something to make him feel better, but how could she help?

Just as she was drifting off to sleep, a brilliant idea came to her.

The next morning at breakfast Olivia told Ian all about a different fairy: the Button Fairy.

"The Button Fairy?" said Ian. "What does she do?"

"Well, you know how buttons get lost really easily, and then they're always very hard to find?" Olivia asked. "If you find a lost button and put it under your pillow for the Button Fairy to take, she'll leave you a little surprise just like the Tooth Fairy does!"

"Really?" said Ian. "Then I'm going to find a button to put under my pillow tonight!"

Luckily, it was Saturday, so Ian had plenty of time to look for lost buttons. He started in what he thought was a very smart place to look: the coat closet. But after searching in every coat pocket and all over the floor, he gave up. Olivia's old winter jacket was missing a button, but he couldn't even find that!

In the laundry room he found a pair of Father's pants that were missing a button, but again, the button itself was nowhere to be found.

He checked under every bed in the house, but still found no buttons.

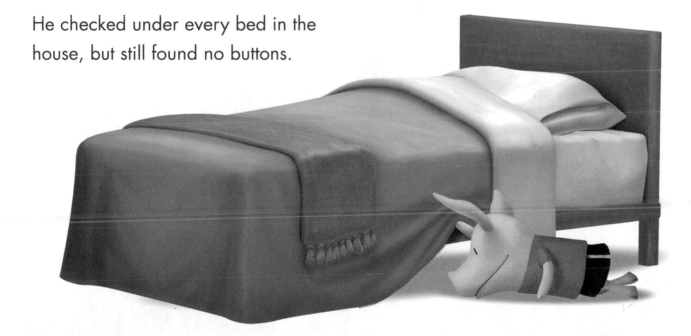

Ian was digging through the couch cushions in the living room when his dad came in.

"Did you lose something, Ian?" Father asked.

"Sort of . . . I'm looking for a lost button," Ian responded.

"Let me help," said Father. He helped Ian search under each couch cushion, and then lifted up the couch so that Ian could look underneath.

"Did you find it?" he asked, panting.

"Nope," said Ian. "Still no buttons."

"I think your mother keeps some buttons in her sewing kit," said Father, setting the couch back down carefully. "You could check there—maybe she has the button you're missing."

Sure enough, Mother's sewing kit had buttons—a whole bag full of them! Ian took the bag and ran excitedly into Olivia's room.

"Look, Olivia. I found lots of buttons! The Button Fairy is going to leave me lots of presents!"

"Wow, that's great, Ian!" Olivia said nervously.

When Ian left, Olivia took out her piggy bank. She shook it upside down and a few coins came out.

"Oh no," she moaned. "What am I going to do? I promised Ian a surprise from the button fairy, but I never thought he would find that many buttons!"

Then, just like the night before, a brilliant idea came to Olivia.

"I know exactly what to give him!" she said, and she got right to work on her plan.

Olivia waited patiently for Ian to go to bed that night. She peeked into his room and watched as he carefully placed all of his buttons underneath his pillow. When he got into bed and turned out the light, she put her plan into action.

First she put on her newly made Button Fairy costume and checked in the mirror to make sure her wings were straight. Then she went down to the kitchen to get Ian's special surprise.

When Olivia was absolutely positive that Ian was asleep, she tiptoed quietly into his room carrying a big brown paper bag. She went to put it under his pillow and quickly realized it was way too big, so she slowly slid it under the bed.

Then she took a piece of paper from Ian's desk and wrote a note that said:

Dear Ian,

Thank you for collecting all these missing buttons for me!

Check under your bed for a very special present.

Love,

The Button Fairy

The first thing Ian did the next morning was check under his pillow. When he saw the note from the Button Fairy, he jumped out of his bed and pulled the brown paper bag out from under it. He opened it to find a whole bunch of . . .

"Apples?" Ian said. "What kind of special present is that?"
"Maybe the Button Fairy had a reason for giving you apples," said
Olivia, appearing in the doorway. "You should at least try one."
Ian shrugged and took a big bite of an apple. "Ah!" he yelled.

"What happened?" asked Olivia.

"My tooth!" shouted Ian. "My tooth came out!" He held it up to show Olivia.

"See," she said. "I knew it would come out soon!"

"I guess the Button Fairy is smarter than I thought she was," said Ian.

"I've heard that she's pretty smart," Olivia agreed.

That night, after helping Ian put his tooth under his pillow, Olivia crawled into her own bed. Mother came in to say good night.

"I'm glad the Tooth Fairy is in charge of Ian's surprise tonight," declared Olivia. "Because I am exhausted!"

Mother laughed. "You're a great big sister, Olivia! Good night."

"Thanks, Mom," said Olivia sleepily. "Good night!"